Hello Night * Hola noche

by / *por* **Amy Costales** Illustrated by / *ilustrado por* **Mercedes McDonald**

www.lunarisingbooks.com

Composed in the United States of America
Printed in China

Edited by Theresa Howell
Designed by David Jenney

FIRST IMPRESSION 2007
ISBN 13: 978-0-87358-927-7
ISBN 10: 0-87358-927-0

11 10 09 08 07 5 4 3 2 1

Library of Congress Cataloging-in-Publication Data

Costales, A. (Amy), 1974-
Hello night = Hola noche / by Amy Costales ; illustrated by
Mercedes McDonald.
p. cm.
Summary: A mother and her baby take a walk before bedtime, greeting
everything they see.
ISBN-13: 978-0-87358-927-7 (hardcover)
ISBN-10: 0-87358-927-0 (hardcover)
[1. Night--Fiction. 2. Bedtime--Fiction. 3. Babies--Fiction. 4. Stories in
rhyme. 5. Spanish language materials--Bilingual.] I. McDonald, Mercedes,
ill. II. Title. III. Title: Hola noche.
PZ73.C67455 2007
[E]--dc22
2006100061

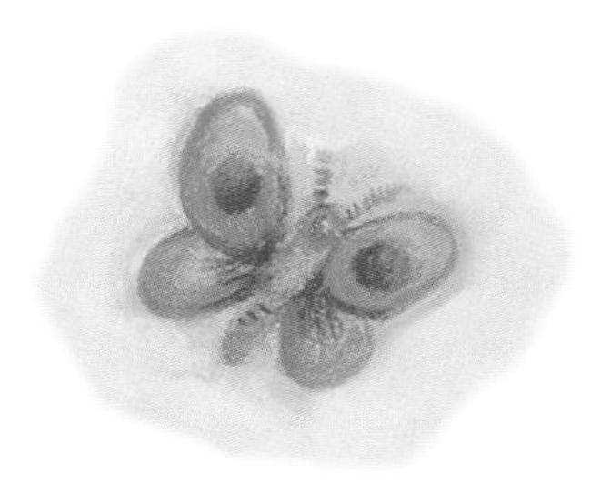

For Sam, who greets the night

A Sam, quien saluda a la noche

—A.C.

For my Jacob, Justin, and Alexandra
and our many walks together

A Jacob, Justin, y Alexandra
y a nuestros inumerables paseos juntos

—M.M.

Hello night. Hello light. Hello stroller, snuggly tight.

Hola noche. Hola carreola. Hola luz de la farola.

Hello night. Hello river. Hello bird with a chirp and a quiver.

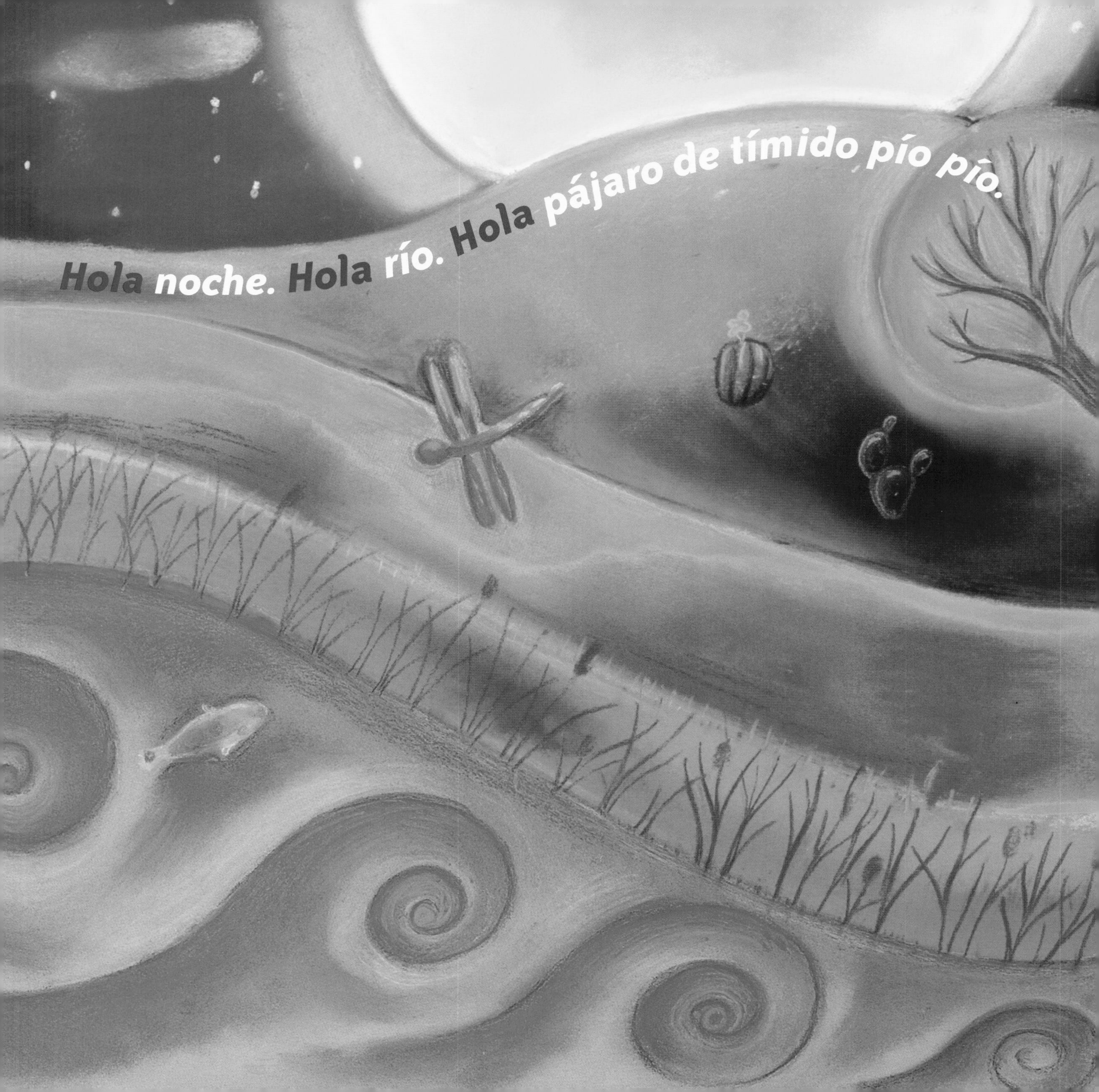

Hola noche. Hola río. Hola pájaro de tímido pío pío.

Hello night.

Hello door. Hello fruit on the orchard floor.

Hola noche.

Hola puerta.

Hola fruta de la huerta.

Hello night. Hello owl. Hello black cat out for a prowl.

Hola noche. Hola tecolote. Hola gato vagabundo y negrote.

Hello night.
Hello cricket. Hello mouse under the thicket.

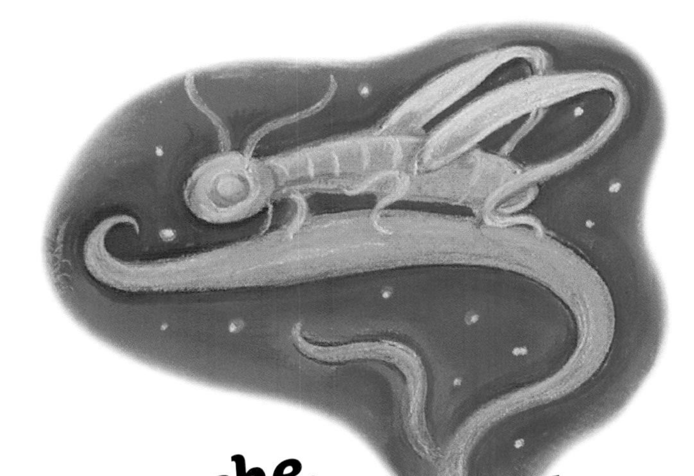

Hola noche.
Hola grillo. Hola arbusto y ratoncillo.

Hello night. Hello moon. Hello sky, dark lagoon.

Hola noche. Hola luna. Hola cielo, grande laguna.

Hello night. Hello tree. Hello stars up above me.

Hola noche. Hola estrellas. Hola árbol de flores tan bellas.

Hello night. Hello home. Hello dog on the roam.

Hola noche. Hola casa. Hola perro que corriendo pasa.

Hello night. **Hello** bed. **Hello** duckies from foot to head.

Hola noche. Hola cama. Hola patitos en mi piyama.

Goodnight night.

It's time to sleep. I close my eyes without a peep.

Buenas noches noche.

Estoy casi dormido. Cierro los ojos sin gemido.